# Kittens in the Kitchen

Swim into more

# PuRRmaiDs

adventures!

# Purrmaids

## Kittens in the Kitchen

by Sudipta Bardhan-Quallen

illustrations by Vivien Wu

A STEPPING STONE BOOK™
Random House 🏠 New York

Text copyright © 2020 by Sudipta Bardhan-Quallen
Cover art copyright © 2020 by Andrew Farley
Interior illustrations copyright © 2020 by Vivien Wu

Random House and the colophon are registered trademarks and A Stepping Stone Book and the colophon are trademarks of Penguin Random House LLC. PURRMAIDS® is a registered trademark of KIKIDOODLE LLC and is used under license from KIKIDOODLE LLC.

Visit us on the Web!
rhcbooks.com

Educators and librarians, for a variety of teaching tools, visit us at RHTeachersLibrarians.com

*Library of Congress Cataloging-in-Publication Data*
Names: Bardhan-Quallen, Sudipta, author. | Wu, Vivien, illustrator.
Title: Kittens in the kitchen / by Sudipta Bardhan-Quallen;
illustrations by Vivien Wu.
Description: First edition. | New York: Random House, [2020] |
Series: Purrmaids; 7 | "A Stepping Stone Book."
Summary: After a field trip to learn about new foods, purrmaid friends Shelly, Angel, and Coral decide to cook a surprise meal for teacher Ms. Harbor and her friend, but unexpected challenges arise.
Identifiers: LCCN 2019002137 | ISBN 978-1-9848-9607-0 (trade pbk.) |
ISBN 978-1-9848-9608-7 (lib. bdg.) | ISBN 978-1-9848-9609-4 (ebook)
Subjects: | CYAC: Mermaids—Fiction. | Cats—Fiction. | Food—Fiction. |
Cooking—Fiction. | School field trips—Fiction.
Classification: LCC PZ7.B25007 Kit 2020 | DDC [Fic]—dc23

Printed in the United States of America
10 9 8 7 6 5 4 3 2 1
First Edition

To Jim,
my personal paw-some chef

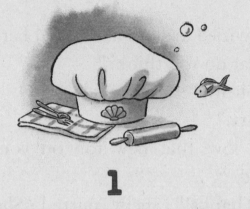

# 1

Shelly thought field trips were one of the most fin-tastic things about sea school. And in Ms. Harbor's class, the trips were even more paw-some. Ms. Harbor was the kind of teacher who knew how to plan something fin-teresting and fun!

Shelly was very particular with the way she dressed. She always tried to look purr-fectly clean and purr-fectly beautiful. When she swam into the kitchen, she twirled around and asked her family, "What do you think?"

"Shelly!" Mom said. "You look so purr-ty."

"I love that new top on you," Dad added.

"Thanks!" Shelly purred. She loved her new green top, too, especially the small silver scallops along the sleeves. They sparkled in the light as Shelly swam around. "I can't wait to show Angel and Coral!"

Angel and Coral were Shelly's two best friends. They did everything together! Even though they didn't look alike, they matched each other every day in a small way. They wore identical friendship bracelets, decorated with all the same charms. Their bracelets were signs of their friendship for the entire ocean to see.

Shelly loved matching her best friends. But she also loved to stand out!

"Hurry up and eat your breakfast," Mom said. She pointed to a plate on the counter.

"Mom made frog egg jelly donuts," Shelly's sister Tempest said.

"Just be careful," her other sister, Gale, warned. "The jelly is really messy! It's all over my paws."

"And your face!" Dad laughed.

Shelly scowled. She said, "I don't want to—"

"Get your clothes dirty!" Her sisters laughed. Everyone knew that Shelly hated messes.

Shelly frowned and began to cook. "I think I'll make scrambled tuna eggs," she said.

Usually, Dad made the scrambled tuna

eggs using his secret ingredient—a sprinkle of sea urchin. Shelly reached for it, but then she saw a mango. "Maybe I'll try something new," she said to herself. She peeled the mango and cut it into small pieces. She carefully avoided the oval pit in the center of the fruit. She added the pieces to her eggs.

When she went to the table with her creation, Mom asked, "What did you make?"

"I thought I'd try something new," Shelly said. "Would anyone like a taste?"

Tempest and Gale frowned at Shelly's mango-and-eggs. They shook their heads.

"That looks weird," Tempest said.

"I don't want to be the first one to try it," Gale said.

Shelly could feel her face getting hot. She didn't think she'd had a bad idea. It hurt that her sisters wouldn't try any.

Then Dad said, "I want some." He popped a spoonful into his mouth. Immediately, he grinned. "This is fin-credible!" he exclaimed. "You invented a brand-new recipe."

Shelly smiled as she ate her breakfast. It wasn't the same as donuts, but her recipe was good. *I'm glad I tried some-thing new,* she thought.

After breakfast, Shelly swam toward Leondra's Square to meet her friends. She saw a black-and-white kitten and an orange kitten from a block away. Angel and Coral were waiting for her. Shelly sped up to reach her friends sooner.

"You're finally here," Angel said. "I thought I was the one who was always late!"

Before Shelly answered, Coral said, "We need to leave! I want to be on time for school."

"Sorry," Shelly said. "I made my own breakfast this morning, so it took a little longer to get ready." She turned toward sea school. "But we can make up some time if we race!"

Soon, the purrmaids were settling

into their desks in Room Eel-Twelve. The morning bell rang, and Ms. Harbor swam to the board. "I'm so excited about today," she purred. "Before the field trip, though, let's talk about your homework."

Some of the students groaned. But Ms. Harbor added, "No homework tonight!"

"No homework!" Baker exclaimed.

"That's the best kind!" Taylor cheered.

"We're visiting Coastline Farm today," Ms. Harbor continued. "We'll learn about the fruits and vegetables that they grow."

Angel scowled. "A farm doesn't sound very . . . exciting," she said.

"You might be surprised," Ms. Harbor answered. "There will be foods there you may not have ever seen. I don't even know recipes for most of them."

Shelly smiled. She already knew she was good at thinking of recipes. Cooking was something that made Shelly really stand out. *I'll figure out some great recipes tonight,* she thought. *Ms. Harbor will be so impressed!*

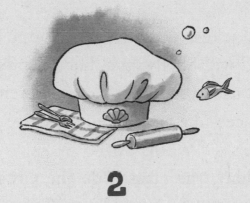

## 2

As the class lined up to leave for the field trip, Shelly leaned over to Coral and Angel. "Maybe I can cook something with the foods we see," she whispered. "With your help, of course."

"That would be paw-some!" Angel replied. "We could teach Ms. Harbor how to use the foods we learn about today."

The purrmaids of Eel-Twelve swam to the Cross Cove Current. It was one of the quickest ways to get around Kitten-tail Cove. Shelly and her friends some-times used the Cross Cove Current to get to places like the Kittentail Cove Science Center.

Today, the class rode the Cross Cove Current past the Science Center. After another two stops, they were at the edge of Kittentail Cove. Ms. Harbor announced, "We're here!"

Shelly looked around. She had been to many farms with her parents to get ingredients for their restaurant. Sea lettuce or sea lemon farms had huge fields for those foods to grow in. Farms for shrimp or sea cucumbers had pens where the animals were raised. But here, Shelly only saw open ocean all around. The water was bright from the sun— except for one large shadowy area.

It looked like there was an island above them.

"This doesn't look like a farm," Shelly whispered to Angel and Coral. "Do you think we came to the wrong stop?"

Coral shrugged. "If Ms. Harbor says we're here, then we must be in the right place."

Ms. Harbor noticed her students' confused faces. "We're not quite at the farm yet," she said. "We have to wait for Mr. Bengal."

"Who's Mr. Bengal?" Angel asked.

Ms. Harbor smiled. "He's an old friend of mine," she purred. "We actually went to sea school together. His family moved to Kittentail Cove from a village in the Indian Ocean when we were kittens."

"And Ms. Harbor was one of my first friends," someone said. A purrmaid with orange-and-black-striped fur floated next to Ms. Harbor.

"Arnab!" Ms. Harbor exclaimed. "It's so nice to see you!"

"You, too, Azurine," Mr. Bengal replied. He gave her a kiss on the cheek. Then he turned to the students. "I was a little surprised that Azurine decided to be a teacher." He grinned. "But I guess after spending so much time in the principal's office, she got used to being at school!"

Shelly gasped. *Ms. Harbor? In trouble at the principal's office?* She couldn't believe it!

"Arnab!" Ms. Harbor yowled. "Don't tell my class that! What will they think of me?" She turned to her students and winked.

"I can't imagine Ms. Harbor in trouble," Coral whispered.

"I can!" Angel giggled.

"Could we get back to the tour, please?" Ms. Harbor asked. She sounded stern. But she was smiling, so Shelly knew her teacher wasn't really upset.

Mr. Bengal nodded. "Welcome to Coastline Farm," he said. "I can't wait to show you all the fin-teresting things we do here!"

Shelly raised her paw. "Mr. Bengal," she said, "where *is* the farm?"

Mr. Bengal laughed. "You were expecting fields of sea lemons or pens of shrimp, weren't you?"

Shelly nodded.

"Coastline Farm is different from the kinds of farms you're used to in Kittentail Cove," Mr. Bengal said. "We don't grow anything underwater."

"What?" asked Angel.

"Where else would you grow things?" Coral asked.

"On land!" Mr. Bengal replied.

"Are you ready to see the farm?" Ms. Harbor asked. The students said yes.

"Follow me!" Mr. Bengal called.

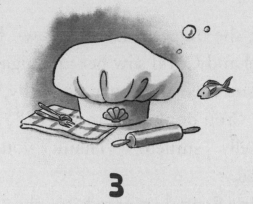

# 3

As the purrmaids got closer to the surface, Shelly noticed the island looked like a donut from below. It was shaped like a circle with a large lagoon in the center. When they reached the lagoon, Mr. Bengal waved for the purrmaids to poke their heads out of the water. "You can even sit on the edge of the lagoon," he said. "Then you'll be able to get a really good view."

Shelly sat on the rocky shore. The first

thing she did was smooth down her fur. Angel and Coral saw her and giggled.

"You look very purr-ty, Shelly," Angel said. "You don't have to worry."

Shelly smiled. "Thank you!" she purred.

Mr. Bengal pointed to the island's outer edge. "Does anyone recognize those trees?" he asked.

Shelly looked over her shoulder. The tall trees had branches filled with large green leaves and bright red and yellow fruit. They grew close together and almost formed a wall around the island.

"Do you know what those are?" Coral whispered to Shelly.

Shelly nodded. She raised her paw. "I think those are mango trees," she said.

"You're correct!" Mr. Bengal exclaimed.

Shelly grinned. "I used mango in my breakfast today."

Angel scratched her head. "How do you reach the mangoes up there?" she asked.

"We wait until they fall off," Mr. Bengal replied. "We have so many trees that there is always some fruit on the sand."

"So this is a mango farm?" Coral asked.

Mr. Bengal shook his head. "We do collect the mangoes," he said. "There's no reason to let them go to waste. But the trees are there so any humans sailing by won't see the purrmaids working on the farm."

"I *thought* it looked like a wall," Shelly purred.

Mr. Bengal pointed to some fenced-in

patches near the lagoon shore. "Those are our fields."

Some of the fields were in the sand near the water's edge. Others were on the rocks that jutted out into the lagoon. "We grow a few kinds of food," Mr. Bengal said. "We mark the different fields with these." He pointed to the small sculptures on the tops of the fence posts.

"They're beautiful," Angel said. She gently touched the nearest sculpture. It looked like a turtle shell.

"Thank you," Mr. Bengal said. "I carve them myself."

Shelly examined one of the sculptures closely. There was something about the shape that was familiar. "Are these mango pits?" she asked.

Mr. Bengal nodded. "You're right again!" He turned to Ms. Harbor. "You have very smart kittens in your class," he said.

"Yes, I do," Ms. Harbor agreed.

There were yellow and brown blobs growing inside the fence with the turtle-shell carvings. They looked a little slimy. "We grow some of our crops right on the rocks," Mr. Bengal said. "These are sea cauliflowers. Has anyone tasted these before?"

Everyone shook their heads.

Mr. Bengal plucked a few blobs off the rocks and passed them out. "Try a piece," he said.

Shelly looked down at the sea cauliflower in her paw. It looked even more slimy up close than it had in the field. She wrinkled her nose. *I don't want to eat this,* she thought.

Angel whispered, "This doesn't look so yummy."

Even Ms. Harbor didn't look eager to taste her piece. She poked at it with a claw, but she didn't put it in her mouth.

"What are you waiting for?" Mr. Bengal asked. "Go ahead."

But no one moved. The smile on Mr. Bengal's face began to fade.

Shelly always got upset when she cooked something new and no one was brave enough to try it. She didn't want Mr. Bengal to feel that way. She also couldn't think of recipes for sea cauliflower without knowing what it tasted like!

Shelly took a deep breath. "I'll go first," she purred.

Mr. Bengal's smile came back. "Thank you for being brave," he said.

Shelly nodded and put a small bite in her mouth. She chewed for a moment. Then she grinned. "This is really good!" she exclaimed.

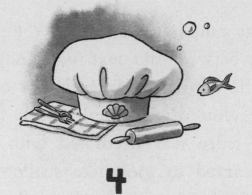

## 4

The students of Eel-Twelve soon agreed that sea cauliflower tasted a lot better than it looked! Angel even asked, "Can I have another piece?"

"I'm glad you kittens like these," Mr. Bengal said. "And I'm glad Shelly had the courage to take the first bite."

"Shelly reminded us all that it's important to try new things," Ms. Harbor added.

The purrmaids swam to the shallow water between the next two sandy fields. On the left, there were clumps of green plants dotted with small purple flowers. That fence was decorated with mango pits carved to look like scallop shells. Plump plants with bright pink flowers grew in the field on the right. The fence around it was decorated with carved fish sculptures.

"These aren't the same plant, are they?" Shelly asked.

Mr. Bengal shook his head. "No, they're not. These," he said, pointing to the side with the scallop-shell fence, "are sea mustard plants." He pointed to the fish sculpture side. "And these are called beach bananas."

This time, the students weren't as

nervous about trying the foods. "I want a beach banana," Coral said.

"I'll have the sea mustard," Angel said.

"I want to try both!" Shelly laughed.

"I think everyone should taste everything," Ms. Harbor said.

Mr. Bengal picked some little green pods off the sea mustard plants. Then he did the same with the dark red beach bananas. He also picked some leaves off the beach banana plants. "You can actually eat the flowers and the stems," he explained, "but the fruit and the leaves are probably easiest to eat."

Each student got a green pod and a red fruit. "Peel the beach banana and eat the fruit inside," Mr. Bengal said. "You can eat the beach banana leaves and the sea mustard pods whole."

Shelly peeled the beach banana and plopped it into her mouth. "This is sweet," she said.

Coral added, "It's a little tangy, too."

Shelly nodded. "Sweet and tangy is a fin-teresting combination," she said.

"It's different," Mr. Bengal agreed. "But that's what makes it special."

"Do the leaves taste the same as the fruit?" Angel asked.

"Taste one and find out," Mr. Bengal replied.

Angel took a bite of a beach banana leaf. "It's salty," she said. "It's very different from the fruit."

Next, it was time to taste the sea mustard. Shelly looked at the little green pod. She shrugged and took a bite. Almost fin-stantly, her eyes grew wide. She spat the pod back into her paw. "This is super spicy!" she exclaimed.

"That's what I love!" Angel said, happily chewing. "Spicy food is fin-tastic!"

"Now that you've tasted all the sea crops we have here, you can swim around the farm to get a second look," Mr. Ben-gal said. "Pick anything you want." He held out some bags that said COASTLINE FARM on them. "Take some food home to try with your families."

"What a generous offer!" Ms. Harbor purred.

"What should we pick, Shelly?" Angel asked.

"Do you know what you want to cook?" Coral asked.

Shelly shrugged. "Not yet. Let's gather a little bit of everything," she said. "Even some mangoes. We can figure out the recipes later."

Angel and Coral nodded. "That's a purr-fect plan," Coral said.

The girls swam off to pick the crops. Angel got two pawfuls of sea mustard. Coral collected some sea cauliflower and a few plump mangoes. Shelly gathered some beach bananas and leaves. She

picked some of the flowers, too. Mom and Dad always decorated their most fancy creations with shells or corals. *Tonight, we can decorate with flowers,* Shelly thought.

Ms. Harbor saw them with their crops. "What are you girls taking home?" she asked.

"Everything!" Shelly said. "We're going to come up with recipes for all of these." Suddenly, she grinned. "I have a great idea!" she exclaimed. "Ms. Harbor, would you like to eat at the Lake Restaurant tonight? We're cooking a special meal using the Coastline Farm crops."

Ms. Harbor smiled. "That would be paw-some," she said. "I love eating at your family's restaurant. Can I bring Mr. Bengal?"

"Of course!" Shelly said. "Come to the restaurant at six o'clock."

"It's a date." Ms. Harbor laughed. "I'll be sure to make a reservation right after school. I can't wait to see what kittens in the kitchen can do!"

# 5

Ms. Harbor swam off to say goodbye to Mr. Bengal. That's when Coral tugged on Shelly's paw. "Are you sure about inviting our teacher?" she asked. "What if we can't make a whole dinner with these foods?"

Shelly gulped. "I didn't think about that," she said. "Should I tell her not to come?"

"No way!" Angel exclaimed. "You're

the best chef we know. You'll be able to think of a whole menu. I believe in you."

"I believe in you, too," Coral said. "I just got worried for a minute." She shrugged. "You know I worry too much."

Shelly smiled. "Thank you both for believing in me," she said. "I think we should spend less time worrying and more time cooking."

"First we have to get home," Angel said.

"Good thing it's time to go!" Shelly exclaimed.

The students of Eel-Twelve returned to the Cross Cove Current. Shelly swam ahead of her classmates.

"Slow down!" Coral called. "You know I don't swim that fast!"

"Even I can't keep up with you!" Angel said.

Shelly stopped and looked over her shoulder. She said, "I'm sorry. I just want to get back quickly." Butterfly fish fluttered in her stomach. *I can't wait to start cooking,* she thought.

"But we all have to stay together," Coral said.

"Coral is right," Ms. Harbor purred. "I know you're excited. But you can't swim away from the class." She winked. "You *can* swim next to me right at the front, though."

It took longer than Shelly wanted, but soon, sea school was up ahead. The purrmaids had just enough time to get back to Eel-Twelve and get their things before the final bell. Shelly placed the bags from the farm carefully inside her backpack. "Let's go," she said. "We have a lot to do."

"Wait a minute," Angel said. There was still a mess on her desk. "I need to put everything away before I leave."

Shelly sighed. Angel was always running late! "Please hurry up."

"Almost done!" Angel answered.

When Angel's desk was clear, Shelly started to leave. But then Coral said, "Wait! I need my library book." She put her bag down and swam to her desk. "It's here somewhere."

Shelly clenched her paws. First Angel was wasting time, and now Coral! "You're not going to have time to read today, Coral."

"I still want it," Coral replied. "It's a cookbook. It might come in handy later."

"A cookbook?" Shelly's eyes grew wide. That could actually be a big help! "I'll search with you," she said.

It took fur-ever to find the book, but Shelly finally did. "Here it is!" Shelly exclaimed, smiling. She looked at the cover. In a fin-stant, her smile disappeared. "This is a human cookbook," she said. Humans and purrmaids had very different ways of cooking. They also used very different ingredients. "We can't use this!" She groaned.

Coral held her backpack open for the book. "It could give us fin-spiration," she said.

Shelly rolled her eyes. Looking for the cookbook had been a waste of time. "Are you two ready now?" she muttered. "I really need to get to work."

"You mean *we* really need to get to work," Angel said. "We're cooking together, right?"

"Of course we are," Coral purred. She wrapped an arm around Shelly's waist. "But Shelly will be in charge. She's a paw-some chef."

Shelly had to smile at that. "Come on, you two," she said. "It's time to get cooking!"

As the girls swam into the restaurant, Shelly said, "Hi, Mom! Hi, Dad!"

Mom looked confused. "What are you

girls doing here?" she asked. "Shouldn't you be doing homework?"

"We don't have any homework tonight, Mrs. Lake," Coral replied.

"We're here to make dinner for our teacher," Angel added. "We brought food from Coastline Farm to cook with."

"We've never tried anything from there," Dad said. "Show us what you have."

Shelly emptied the bags onto the kitchen counter.

"I know those are mangoes," Mom said, "but I've never seen the rest of these!"

"We hadn't, either!" Coral exclaimed.

Shelly pointed to the different foods. "These are sea cauliflower, sea mustard, and beach bananas."

Mom scratched her head. "I've never cooked with those," she said.

"That's why I have to think of new recipes," Shelly said.

"That's a challenge," Dad said.

"Shelly is up for it!" Angel exclaimed. "She always knows just what to cook."

Shelly bit her lip. She felt the butterfly fish in her stomach again. Coral and Angel were both excited now. But Shelly was getting nervous. *What if I can't think of a good idea?*

# 6

"Before you girls get started," Mom said, "you should have a snack. I made my famous Garden Urchin Roll."

Dad brought out a tray of sushi. The girls plopped pieces into their mouths. "This is so good," Coral purred.

"What's in this again?" Angel asked.

"Sea cucumber, sea lettuce, sea grapes, and sea urchin," Dad answered, "wrapped in seaweed." He grinned. "You can *sea* why they're fin-credible!"

Shelly groaned. "That's such a dad joke!"

"Well," Dad said, "I *am* your father."

When the girls had finished their snack, Shelly floated over to the foods from Coastline Farm. "I have an idea for a recipe," she said. She gathered things from around the kitchen. "We need some chopped sea urchin and sliced sea cucumber. Maybe a sprinkle of sea grapes. And a few sheets of seaweed." She swam to the sea mustard. "Let's use this, too."

"What are you planning?" Coral asked.

"A new sushi hand roll," Shelly replied. She chopped a few sea mustard pods into little pieces. She arranged some sea mustard, sea cucumber, and sea urchin on the seaweed sheets. She wrapped each one into a cone. Then she sprinkled some sea grapes on top. She held two cones out to her friends. "Would you like to try a spicy sea mustard hand roll?"

Coral and Angel bit into their sushi rolls. Angel smiled. "It's good!" she said.

But Coral was frowning. "Don't you like it, Coral?" Shelly asked.

"It's great," Coral said. "But isn't this just a Garden Urchin Roll with some sea mustard? It doesn't seem like a new recipe."

Now Shelly frowned. "I guess you're right," she said. "I didn't even think about that."

"It's all right!" Angel said. "We just need more fin-spiration."

"We could make a sushi roll with mangoes and shrimp," Coral suggested.

Shelly shook her head. "My parents already make a mango and shrimp sushi roll."

"Maybe we could prepare a seafood salad with sea cauliflower," Angel said.

"No," Shelly said. "That won't be very different, either. I want to try to make foods that purrmaids don't eat all the time."

"Should we check Coral's cookbook for ideas?" Angel asked.

"That's for making human food," Shelly said. "We probably can't use any ideas from there." She stared at the Coastline Farm foods again. "This is harder than I thought it would be."

"What's harder?" Dad asked, swimming up behind Shelly.

Shelly sighed. "I wanted to think of brand-new recipes," she said.

"But all your ideas sound like things purrmaids already eat all the time?" Dad asked.

Shelly frowned. "How did you know?"

Dad pulled her into a hug and

whispered, "Fathers are good at reading their daughters' minds." He kissed Shelly's forehead. "You girls should know that most recipes are inspired by familiar foods," he said. "There are two ways that chefs make foods seem really different from the same old meals. One way is to mix flavors in different ways."

"Like mixing something spicy with something really sweet?" Shelly asked.

Dad nodded. "That actually sounds like it might taste fin-tastic," he said.

"What's the other thing chefs do?" Coral asked.

"We change the way something is cooked," Dad said. "Here at the restaurant, we use our oven a lot. That makes food taste completely different from what purrmaids expect."

Suddenly, Shelly's eyes grew wide. "I

can't believe I didn't think of this before!" she purred. "The *oven* is our secret ingredient!"

Cooking in Kittentail Cove was a little tricky. On land, humans used fire to heat and cook their food. But fire didn't really work underwater! So cooking for most purrmaids involved chopping, seasoning, spicing, and mixing. But at the restaurant, the Lakes were able to do more—because they had an oven.

Mom and Dad chose a special location for the restaurant. It was built over an opening in the ocean floor called a thermal vent. The water that came out of a thermal vent was very hot—sometimes hundreds of degrees! The Lakes built a long tunnel over the thermal vent that reached almost to the surface of the water. That way, the heated water didn't hurt

anyone. But the tunnel ran through the Lake Restaurant kitchen—and it made a wonderful oven for cooking.

Shelly waved for her friends to come over to the large metal door on the far side of the kitchen. "I finally have my first really good idea," she said. "We'll use the oven to cook something special!"

# 7

"I've never used an oven before," Angel said.

"I'll show you how," Shelly said.

"With my help," Dad said. He floated next to his daughter. "The oven is a wonderful machine, but it's only safe if you follow the rules."

"Rules?" Coral asked. "What are they? I want to be sure we're following all of them. Should we take notes?"

Shelly and Angel looked at each other and shook their heads. Coral was always worried about following the rules.

Dad patted Coral's shoulder. "No need for notes. You girls just need a grown-up to keep an eye on you."

Coral let out a deep breath and nodded.

Shelly kissed Dad's cheek and said, "We'll tell you when we're ready for help." She opened a cabinet under the counter and looked inside. "We need the oven pans first."

"What are those?" Angel asked.

Shelly took out some covered metal pans with long handles. "Anything we want to cook in the oven needs to go into

one of these oven pans," she explained. "We put the food inside and close the lid tightly. That way, when the hot water from the thermal vent flows up, it doesn't take our meal along for the ride!"

"That makes sense," Coral said. "These foods were grown on land, but we don't want to send them back up!"

"Exactly!" Shelly exclaimed.

"What do you want us to do first?" Angel asked.

"I like the idea of mixing something spicy with something sweet," Shelly replied. "Let's cook sea mustard and mangoes with shrimp. We can fry everything in fish oil so it's crispy."

"That sounds like a fin-tastic main dish," Angel said. "Can I have the first bite?"

Shelly rolled her eyes. "Maybe, Angel,"

she joked. She pointed to the beach bananas. "These are so sweet and tangy," she said. "We could make a pie with a kelp crust."

"That would be a paw-some dessert," Coral said.

"What about the sea cauliflower?" Angel asked. "Or the beach banana leaves? Do you have an idea for those?"

Shelly scratched her head. "I think we could roast the sea cauliflower and beach banana leaves," she said. "We can mix it with chopped sea urchins and serve it over sea lettuce. It will be a new type of seafood salad."

"That's a purr-fect appetizer!" Coral exclaimed.

"You came up with a whole menu, Shelly," Angel said.

Shelly smiled. "I only came up with

the *ideas* for the menu," she purred. "If we want to have food, we'd better get to work!"

Shelly passed Angel the beach bananas. "You can chop these into small pieces," she said. She pushed the mangoes toward Coral. "Peel these and slice them, please," she said. "Be careful around the pits! I'm going to make the pie crust." She lined a pie pan with a piece of seaweed and placed it inside an oven pan. "This is ready for baking."

"I'm done chopping," Angel said.

"And I'm done slicing," Coral said.

"Angel, bring me a bowl of shrimp from over there," Shelly said, pointing. "Coral, bring me your mango slices and those sea mustard pods."

Angel and Coral grabbed the supplies. Shelly showed them how to put everything

in an oven pan. "One piece of mango, one mustard pod, one piece of shrimp," she said. "Then repeat!"

The purrmaids worked quickly. They used all the shrimp. Coral asked, "Should we save some of the shrimp for something else?"

Shelly shook her head. "We have a saying here at the restaurant: *When you cook a meal with shrimp, don't you even try to skimp!*"

Coral giggled. "I guess purrmaids do like to eat shrimp."

Shelly added some fish oil to the pan and sealed it up. "This is ready for the oven."

"What's next?" Angel asked.

"We can roast the vegetables together in one pan," Shelly said. The girls filled the largest oven pan with all the sea cauliflower and beach banana leaves.

"We should make a saying for this dish, too," Coral said. "How about this? *When you cook a meal of veggies, fill the pan up to the . . . edgies.*"

The girls giggled. "That's not as catchy as Shelly's saying," Angel joked.

Shelly sprinkled a little fish oil on the vegetables. Then Angel put the lid on the pan.

"Now we need to make the pie filling," Coral said.

"We saved the best for last!" Angel purred.

"This one is easy," Shelly said. She grabbed the smallest oven pan. "We'll roast the beach bananas by themselves so they're nice and soft."

The girls put all the chopped beach bananas into the pan, and Shelly sealed it. Then she did a flip in the water as she shouted for her dad. "We're ready for the oven now!"

# 8

Dad inspected the oven pans. "You girls did a great job with these," he purred. He carefully placed them inside the oven. "Do you know how long you want to cook each dish?"

Shelly looked at the clock again. It was four-thirty. "The pie filling should cook quickly," she said. "I think just twenty minutes. The shrimp dish will take a little longer."

"Like half an hour?" Angel asked.

Shelly nodded. "The roasted vegetables need about forty-five minutes."

"So they come out at five-fifteen," Coral said.

"That leaves just enough time to get everything ready before Ms. Harbor and Mr. Bengal arrive," Shelly said.

"That's a lot to keep track of," Dad said. "You should set a timer."

Shelly shook her head. "We'll be paying attention."

Dad shrugged. "If you say so," he said. "Call me when you want everything taken out."

"What are we going to do while the food is cooking?" Coral asked.

Shelly shrugged. "I guess we could clean up." But there wasn't much to put away. The girls had used almost all the

food from the farm. The only things left
were a few mangoes.

"I have a better idea!" Angel exclaimed.
"Let's look through Coral's cookbook."
She winked. "That's so much more fun
than cleaning."

"And I could use a break," Coral said.
"Being a chef is really hard work."

Shelly grinned. "I guess we earned it."

Coral laid the cookbook open on the counter and flipped through the pages. She pointed to a recipe called Avocado and Herring Dip. "This one looks paw-some."

"*This tastes great with toasted chips,*" Angel read. "*Scoop some dip on a chip and enjoy.*"

"We have herring at the restaurant," Shelly said, "but I've never heard of avocado."

"Humans eat weird things." Coral giggled.

"Look at this," Angel said. She pointed to a chapter called "Making Jelly at Home." "I love frog egg jelly donuts."

"Me too!" Shelly replied. "My family had them for breakfast. Do humans eat frog egg jelly?"

"It doesn't look like it," Angel said. "There's a recipe using strawberries and one using raspberries." She scowled. "What's a berry?"

Coral shrugged. "Maybe it's a type of animal. You never know with humans."

Shelly turned the page. Her eyes grew wide. "There's a recipe for mango jelly! That would have been purr-fect today," she said.

"See?" Coral said. "This cookbook could have been useful."

"It's more than useful," Angel purred. She flipped to another chapter called "Main Courses." "It's actually purr-ty fin-teresting."

Shelly reached for Coral's paw. "I'm glad you made us find it."

Coral blushed. "Most of the recipes wouldn't work for purrmaids," she replied. "But it's fun to learn about them."

The purrmaids reached a recipe called

Mango and Mustard Beef Curry. "That sounds familiar," Shelly said.

"The mango and mustard do," Angel said. "But what's a beef?"

Shelly shrugged. "We can look that up the next time we go to the library," she suggested.

"Yes," Coral agreed, "next time."

Suddenly, Shelly yelped, "Time!" She spun toward the clock so fast that she knocked the cookbook off the counter. "I forgot to check the time!" she wailed. It was five-thirty already. "Everything has been in the oven too long!"

Both of Shelly's parents hurried over. "What happened?" Mom asked.

Shelly felt tears welling in her eyes. "We were reading Coral's cookbook," she said. "I lost track of time, and now everything is ruined!"

Mom put on her oven mitts and took the pans out. She set them on the counter. She opened each pan, then floated back so everyone could see.

The shrimp was nicely fried. But the mangoes and mustard pods had melted into a sticky goo. The seaweed pie crust was so crispy that pieces broke off with a snap. The vegetables were soft and mushy. And the beach bananas had turned into a thick gel.

"These might be overcooked," Angel said.

"Maybe just a little bit," Coral added.

Shelly clenched her paws. "Why didn't you make me set the timer, Dad?" she cried.

Dad squeezed Shelly's paw. "Because sometimes mistakes are the best way to learn," he replied.

"But this mistake ruined everything!" Shelly said.

"Can you make something else?" Mom asked. "Something simpler? And maybe just one dish instead of three?"

Shelly shook her head. "We used up all the Coastline Farm food," she said. She pointed to the clock. "Besides, there's no time to cook something new." She covered her face with her paws. "What are we going to do?"

# 9

Coral and Angel floated to Shelly. "We can still figure something out," Coral purred.

Shelly frowned. "This is all ruined, and I don't have any more ideas." She squeezed her eyes shut to keep the tears from falling. "You shouldn't have put me in charge. I'm really sorry."

"We weren't paying attention to the time, either," Angel said.

"It's our mistake, too," Coral said.

"Something might seem like a mistake," Mom said, "but it might actually be an unexpected opportunity." She turned to the counter. "Let's have a taste of some of these."

"Why?" Shelly asked. "They're overcooked and ruined."

Mom dipped a spoon into the pan that held the mix of melted mango, sea mustard, and shrimp. "This is really yummy," she said. She held the pan out to the girls.

Shelly took a small bite. "You're right, Mom."

Coral scooped up a bit of the mixture and tried it. "It tastes exactly like we wanted it to," she said. "Spicy and sweet."

Angel took one of the cooked shrimp and dunked it in the pan. "It's really good with the shrimp," she said. "It reminds me of the beef recipe we saw in the human cookbook."

Shelly's head snapped up. She darted over to the cookbook.

"What are you doing?" Coral asked.

Shelly pointed at a page. "Angel is right!" she exclaimed. "We didn't mean to, but we basically cooked mango-and-mustard curry."

"Just with shrimp instead of a beef!" Angel said excitedly.

"We can serve this for dinner, after all!" Coral laughed.

"Good thinking, Shelly!" Mom exclaimed. "I told you this could be an opportunity."

"Aren't you glad I didn't make you set a timer?" Dad joked.

Shelly scowled at him, but only for a second. She quickly opened the cabinet that held the restaurant's fanciest silver dishes. They were decorated with starfish and seashells. She spooned all the curry from the pan into one of the dishes. Then she added a few purple sea-mustard flowers around the rim of the dish. "Purr-fect," she said.

"Can we save some of the other things we cooked?" Coral asked. She picked up a fork and took a bite from the pan of sea vegetables. "These are overcooked, but they're still good."

Angel took the fork and tasted the vegetables. She said, "They're just a little mushy."

Shelly swam back to the cookbook. "I bet we can make a vegetable dip with them," she said. She reached for the kelp pie crust and snapped off a piece. "We already made chips!"

Angel started to mash the vegetables. Shelly grabbed some chopped sea urchin. "We can still mix these in," she said.

Coral arranged some sea lettuce on another fancy dish. Then Shelly scooped the urchin-and-vegetable dip on top of the sea lettuce. Angel broke the kelp crust into small chips and placed them around the dip.

Shelly's finishing touch was a beach banana flower. "This one is ready, too."

"What do we do with this?" Angel asked. She held up the pan that was supposed to be the pie filling. The fruits had cooked down to a small amount of sticky gel at the bottom of the pan.

Coral dipped a spoon into the gel to taste it. "It's sweet," she said.

Shelly paged through the cookbook. "I think we cooked beach banana jelly by accident!" But then she pointed to the pan and frowned. "There isn't much here, though. We can't make two desserts out of this little jelly."

"Listen to this," Angel purred. She read, "*Jellies are delicious served on crackers or slices of toast. If you want something sweet, you can pair fruit jelly with cheese or drizzle it over ice cream.*" She stopped and scowled. "All that sounds great, but we don't have crackers, cheese, or ice cream. I don't even know what some of that stuff is!"

Shelly glanced all around the kitchen. "We don't have slices of toast," she said.

"Whatever that is," Angel mumbled.

Then Shelly spotted the extra mangoes that the purrmaids hadn't cooked. "But we can slice this mango," she continued. She quickly peeled one of the fruits and cut it. She put a small scoop of the jelly on each slice. "How do they taste with a bit of beach banana jelly?" she asked.

Angel and Coral each took a bite. They smiled. "This is simple," Coral said.

"But fin-credible!" Angel finished.

"Can I taste some?" Mom asked. Shelly fixed her a piece. Mom said, "I might like this more than coconut pie!"

Angel gasped. "Nothing is better than your coconut pie!"

Everyone laughed.

Shelly finished cutting the mangoes. Angel arranged the slices on a fancy dish. Coral spooned some jelly on each one.

"Do you want to decorate this plate, too?" Angel asked. "We still have some flowers."

"I have a better idea," Shelly said. She took a scrap of mango peel and used the knife to cut it into the shape of a heart.

"Paw-some!" exclaimed Coral and Angel together.

The clock tower at Cove Council Hall chimed six times. Dad poked his head through the kitchen door. "Your guests have arrived," he said.

"We finished just in time," Shelly said. She turned to her friends. "Ready?"

"Definitely!" Coral replied.

But Mom said, "Not quite yet."

Shelly scowled. "What do you mean?"

"You can't just plop brand-new recipes on a table," Mom said. She went to a cabinet and took out three shiny dome lids.

"You don't want anyone to get a sneak peek of your creations!" She grinned and placed a lid over each dish. "Now you're ready."

Shelly gulped. *It's meow or never,* she thought. *I hope this isn't a cat-tastrophe!*

# 10

Shelly picked up the dish with the shrimp curry. Coral grabbed the vegetable dip and kelp chips. Angel took the mango with beach banana jelly.

Shelly looked at her reflection in the shiny lid she was carrying. She felt her paws trembling. She forced herself to smile.

The girls swam out to greet Ms. Harbor and Mr. Bengal. Shelly said, "Thank

you for coming to dinner." She bit her lip. "I hope you'll like what we cooked."

"It smells fin-tastic," Ms. Harbor said. "But why are there three plates for two of us?"

"We made three different recipes," Coral said.

"An appetizer, a main course, and a dessert," Angel added.

"You girls put a lot of work into this," Mr. Bengal said.

"I can't wait to see this feast!" Ms. Harbor purred.

Shelly nodded at Coral and Angel. The purrmaids took the lids off the plates at the same time. "Dinner is served!" Shelly exclaimed.

"Tell us what you've cooked," Mr. Bengal said.

Coral pointed to her dish. "For your

appetizer, we've made an urchin-and-vegetable dip using sea cauliflower and beach banana leaves," she said.

"There is chopped sea urchin mixed in," Shelly explained, "and we've served it with some sea lettuce."

Angel picked up a kelp chip. "You can use these chips to scoop the dip," she said. "They're made from kelp that we baked."

"Next," Shelly said, "there's mango-and-mustard curry with shrimp."

"It's spicy and sweet at the same time," Coral said.

"Finally," Angel said, "these are mango slices topped with beach banana jelly."

"That's the dessert," Shelly purred.

"This is very impressive, girls," Ms. Harbor said. "I'm so proud of you."

"Don't say that until you've tasted everything," Shelly joked.

"It doesn't matter what any of these dishes taste like," Ms. Harbor said. She reached out and squeezed her students' paws. "I'm proud that you three took on this challenge and tried something new. That takes a lot of courage."

"Thank you, Ms. Harbor," Angel said. "But Coral and I couldn't have done this without Shelly. She was in charge of everything."

"Shelly could have made this whole meal without us," Coral said, "but we needed her."

"No, I needed *you*," Shelly said. "And now it's time for you, Ms. Harbor and Mr. Bengal, to take on the challenge."

"What challenge?" Mr. Bengal asked.

"Trying all this new food!" Shelly exclaimed.

Everyone laughed. Then Ms. Harbor asked, "Will you three join us?"

Shelly's mouth fell open. "Do you want us to?"

"Of course!" Ms. Harbor said. "Good food is meant to be shared."

Shelly, Angel, and Coral pulled chairs over to the table. Ms. Harbor spooned some mango-and-mustard curry onto her plate. Mr. Bengal took a few chips and scooped up some of the urchin-and-vegetable dip. Angel reached for a piece of mango with beach banana jelly.

"Angel!" Coral gasped. "You can't start with dessert. It's against the rules!"

Angel took a bite and winked. "You know I don't like to follow the rules."

Everyone laughed again.

Mom floated behind Shelly. "I'd love to hear what you think of the food," she purred. "The girls worked very hard this afternoon."

"It's just fin-tastic!" Ms. Harbor replied. "I don't know which one is my favorite."

"You'll have to add these all to the restaurant menu," Mr. Bengal said.

Mom nodded. "That's our plan!"

"How did you girls think up these delicious recipes?" Mr. Bengal asked.

"It was a bit of an accident," Shelly admitted.

"A happy accident," Coral added.

The girls told the story of their cooking adventure. When they were finished, Mr. Bengal said, "You three are certainly very special purrmaids. You tried something new, and you didn't let mistakes stop you. It took me a lot longer to be that brave." He reached into his pocket and pulled out three small beads. "These are to thank you for inviting me. I hope you like them."

Shelly took one of the beads. It was

carved with the same scallop design as her new top. It also looked very familiar.

"Are these made from mango pits?" she asked.

Mr. Bengal smiled. "I carved them this afternoon."

"They're so purr-ty," Angel said.

"We can wear them on our bracelets," Coral said.

"That's a wonderful plan," Ms. Harbor said. "Every time you see them, you'll be reminded to try something new."

Shelly grinned and took a slice of mango. "And they'll remind us to save room for dessert!"

# Celebrate the paw-lidays with the Purrmaids!

Read on for a sneak peek!

Every year, purrmaids all around Kittentail Cove decorated their town to spread Fish-mas spirit. They carved ice sculptures of Santa Paws and Jack Furr-ost. They made ornaments out of shells to decorate Fish-mas sea fans in their homes.

Most of the Fish-mas sea fans in Kittentail Cove were about as tall as a grownup purrmaid. But there were always two giant sea fans in town. One was in front of the Kittentail Cove Library. The other one was at Coral's house.

"Are you going to get the biggest Fish-mas sea fan you can find?" Shrimp asked.

Papa grinned. "I always do, don't I?"

Shrimp looked down at his letter. "How will I get this to Santa Paws?" he whined.